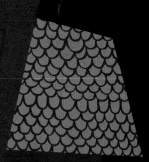

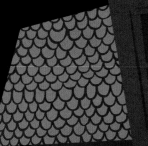

HALLOW'S EVE

The wind is howling;
the leaves are blowing.
A sliver of moon
is barely showing.
The whistling wind
plays an eerie song
while unknown fiends
cast shadows long.
And goblins, ghosts,
and other ghouls
haunt the dark,
where terror rules.
With shrieks and howls
and make-believe,
let's prowl the night—
it's Hallow's Eve!

TRICK -OR- TREAT

A Happy Haunter's Halloween

Debbie Leppanen   Illustrated by **Tad Carpenter**

Beach Lane Books • New York London Toronto Sydney New Delhi

THE SHADOW

I was followed
by something close.
Something dark
and quite morose.
Just my shadow,
nothing to fear.
Until I left . . .
and it stayed here.

COLD BONES

Can anybody tell me
(if anybody knows)
why skeletons aren't freezing
when they don't wear any clothes?

HALLOWEEN PARTY

I raffled my hat.
Whoever did win it
got something extra—
my head was still in it.

SLICK RIDE

Witches on broomsticks
fly over treetops.
Except when it rains,
then they use mops!

NOISES

I heard a noise—
I *think* I did.
Could just be the garbage lid.
I hear a squeak,
could be a mouse.
We get them sometimes in our house.
I hear a creak
out in the hall.
Could just be my cat, Snowball.
I hear a growl
right near my face.
Maybe I should leave this place.
I hear a scream,
could it be . . .
Wait, that noise came from *me*!

SQUEAKY CLEAN

There once was a specter named John
who bathed from dusk until dawn.
When he finally got out,
he let out a shout:
"I've scrubbed so hard that I'm gone!"

MUMMY DEAREST

She fixes my breakfast: worms on toast.
I like the juicy ones the most.

She tears my clothes all to shreds.
(On the bus, it sure turns heads.)

She packs me spider eggs for lunch.
Mmm . . . the way they snap and crunch!

She draws my bath with mud and ice,
then rubs me down with tickly lice.

She reads my favorite horror story
and makes up extra parts—real gory.

She tucks me in and gnaws my tummy.
She spoils me rotten. I love my mummy!

GRAVEYARD

I'm very scared, and I mean *very*,
in this cold, dark cemetery.
It's not the cold that chills my bones;
I'm shivering from these tombstones.
I've read them all and now I'm done.
I've seen *my* name on every one.

DINNER FOR ONE

I eat spiders.
I eat slugs.
I eat any
kind of bugs.
I eat cats
and doggies too.
I eat rats
(they're fun to chew).

I eat grown-ups
by the bunch.
I ate six
today at lunch.
I'm a ghoul,
that's what I do.
Don't ask me home
or I'll eat you!

A VAMPIRE MAKES A WONDERFUL DADDY BECAUSE...

1. He'll let you stay up late at night.
2. He'll wrap you in his cape real tight.
3. You can fly with him in the full moonlight.
4. When someone picks on you, he'll bite!

TRICK-OR-TREAT

Knock, knock.
Is that a mask?
Close the door
and just don't ask.

THE MONSTER

I looked for the monster
under the bed.
I checked my closet
with some dread.
Behind my bureau,
under the chair;
I was delighted
he wasn't there.
I brushed my teeth
before I read.
(I never did check
on top of my head.)

BLACK CAT

The witch complained
that she was green.

The ghost complained
that he was white.

The cat cried out,
"At least *you're* seen,
and not swallowed up
by night."

HAPPY HAUNTER

A shutter bangs;
a floorboard creaks.
This night of gloom
belongs to freaks—
skulking monsters,
swooping bats,
skulls and ghouls
and witches' cats.
But from the covers
I poke my head.
They won't get me.
I'm safe in bed!

For Matt and Maria,
my two favorite treats—D. L.

For Jessica—
you love to scare me and I love that about you!—T. C.

BEACH LANE BOOKS • An imprint of Simon & Schuster Children's Publishing Division • 1230 Avenue of the Americas, New York, New York 10020 • Text copyright © 2013 by Debbie Leppanen • Illustrations copyright © 2013 by Tad Carpenter • All rights reserved, including the right of reproduction in whole or in part in any form. • BEACH LANE BOOKS is a trademark of Simon & Schuster, Inc. • For information about special discounts for bulk purchases, please contact Simon & Schuster Special Sales at 1-866-506-1949 or business@simonandschuster.com. • The Simon & Schuster Speakers Bureau can bring authors to your live event. For more information or to book an event, contact the Simon & Schuster Speakers Bureau at 1-866-248-3049 or visit our website at www.simonspeakers.com. • Book design by Lauren Rille • The text for this book is set in Memphis. • The illustrations for this book are rendered digitally. • Manufactured in China • 0513 SCP
First Edition
2 4 6 8 10 9 7 5 3 1
Library of Congress Cataloging-in-Publication Data
Leppanen, Debbie.
Trick-or-treat : a happy haunter's Halloween / Debbie Leppanen ; illustrated by Tad Carpenter.—1st ed.
p. cm.
ISBN 978-1-4424-3398-4 (hardcover)
ISBN 978-1-4424-3399-1 (eBook)
1. Halloween—Juvenile poetry. I. Carpenter, Tad. II. Title.
PS3612.E63T75 2013
811'.6—dc23
2012004906